GIRLS SURVIVE

Published by Stone Arch Books, an imprint of Capstone
1710 Roe Crest Drive, North Mankato, Minnesota 56003
capstonepub.com

Library of Congress Cataloging-in-Publication Data
Names: Smith, Nikki Shannon, 1971– author. | Jenai, Markia, illustrator.
Title: Lena and the burning of Greenwood : a Tulsa Race Massacre survival story /
by Nikki Shannon Smith ; [illustrated by Markia Jenai]. Other titles: Girls survive.
Description: North Mankato, Minnesota : Stone Arch Books, an imprint of Capstone
[2022] | Series: Girls survive | Audience: Ages 8–12. | Audience: Grades 4–6. |
Summary: Twelve-year-old Lena is aware of racism, but she lives a comfortable life
in the segregated but relatively wealthy Greenwood District in Tulsa, Oklahoma;
but on May 31, 1921 racial tensions explode, and men from downtown Tulsa invade
Greenwood, set on killing and destroying the district—and as the violence escalates
Lena, her parents, and her older sister search desperately for a safe place to hide
from the mob.
Identifiers: LCCN 2021033200 (print) | LCCN 2021033201 (ebook) |
ISBN 9781663990563 (hardcover) | ISBN 9781666329445 (paperback) |
ISBN 9781666329452 (pdf)
Subjects: LCSH: African American families—Oklahoma—Tulsa—Juvenile fiction.
| Tulsa Race Massacre, Tulsa, Okla., 1921—Juvenile fiction. | Massacres—
Oklahoma—History—20th century—Juvenile fiction. | African American
neighborhoods—Oklahoma—Tulsa—History—20th century—Juvenile fiction.
| Greenwood (Tulsa, Okla.)—History—20th century—Juvenile fiction. | Tulsa
(Okla.)—History—20th century—Juvenile fiction. | CYAC: Tulsa Race Massacre,
Tulsa, Okla., 1921—Fiction. | African Americans—Fiction. | Race relations—Fiction.
| Survival—Fiction. | Tulsa (Okla.)—History—20th century—Fiction. | LCGFT:
Historical fiction.
Classification: LCC PZ7.S6566 Le 2022 (print) | LCC PZ7.S6566 (ebook) | DDC
813.6 [Fic]—dc23
LC record available at https://lccn.loc.gov/2021033200
LC ebook record available at https://lccn.loc.gov/2021033201

Editorial Credits
Editor: Alison Deering; Designer: Kay Fraser;
Production Specialist: Katy LaVigne

Image Credits: Shutterstock: Amovitania (geometric background),
Max Lashcheuski (background texture)

LENA AND THE BURNING OF GREENWOOD

A Tulsa Race Massacre Survival Story

by Nikki Shannon Smith

illustrated by Markia Jenai

STONE ARCH BOOKS
a capstone imprint

FOREWORD

The Tulsa Race Massacre was perhaps the most violent, deadly, and devastating crime committed by Americans, against Americans, in history. But somehow, 100 years later, many people have never heard of it.

Turning this event into a work of fiction was a challenge for many reasons. Researching the Tulsa Race Massacre was heartbreaking. I cried almost every time I wrote a scene. I also worried about fictionalizing something so horrifying. For readers, the book might feel like an action-packed adventure. For the citizens of Greenwood, it felt like living a nightmare.

Sadly, the hatred and racism that fueled this massacre still exist today. Some people still find excuses to commit acts of violence against fellow Americans based on their race, religion, and other identities. Often, just like those who attacked Greenwood, the people who commit these crimes go unpunished.

In 2020 and 2021, as news story after news story *showed* Black people senselessly losing their lives, the rest of the world had its eyes opened. People began to truly understand what Black Americans have always experienced. People began to *feel* it. The truth was obvious and ugly.

But the truth must always be told. Our eyes must remain open. Our voices must rise. We must stop history from repeating itself. And so, I tell you this story: a work of fiction with the ugly truth woven into every word and the beauty and strength of Black people present on every page. The people of Greenwood mattered. Their truth—America's truth—cannot be buried with the victims.

"Maybe if we talk about it enough, it'll never be again."
–Ernestine Alpha Gibbs, *Tulsa Race Massacre survivor*

CHAPTER ONE

Greenwood, Oklahoma
Memorial Day
May 30, 1921
9:00 a.m.

I stood at the living room window and stared up at the dark gray clouds in the sky. *Moody.* That's what the weather was.

I'd been hoping for a sunny Memorial Day. I'd been hoping Mama and Daddy might surprise me and my big sister, Cora, with a trip to downtown Tulsa for the Memorial Day parade.

Looks like the only surprise will be rain, I thought.

Daddy came into view from the side of the house where he had been trimming the roses. He smiled and waved at me. Daddy loved his roses.

"Mama," I called, still staring out the window, "do you think they'll still have the parade even if it rains?"

In the kitchen, Mama shut off the faucet. A few seconds later, she appeared in the living room. "I don't know, Lena. Probably."

Cora, who sat in an arm hair in the corner of the living room, closed the book on her lap. She kept her finger in there to mark her page. Cora's nose was always in a book.

"I bet they will," she said.

I looked over at her. I hadn't realized she was listening, but I hoped she was right.

Just then, Daddy came in through the front door. He handed Mama some fresh cut roses.

I sighed. "I wish we could go."

"Go where?" asked Daddy.

"To the Memorial Day parade," I said.

I had never been to downtown Tulsa. In fact, I had never left Greenwood. The only things I knew about life outside the Greenwood District were the things I had heard from my friends at school.

My parents glanced at each other. Sometimes I thought they had a secret eyeball language only they understood. I waited for one of them to say something.

"There's nothing for us in downtown Tulsa," said Mama finally. "No shops open to us and no bathrooms we can use. Black people are second-class citizens there."

I frowned. I knew Tulsa was segregated, but I was still curious. I wanted to see it at least once.

"We have everything we need right here in Greenwood," Daddy added. "No need to go anywhere else. We have our own little slice of America." He chuckled. "That's why Booker T. Washington called it Negro Wall Street."

Even though I hadn't seen anything but Greenwood, I knew it was special. The entire

Greenwood District was about thirty-five blocks and had some of everything. We had our own schools and libraries, hotels, restaurants, a skating rink, a theater, a post office, and even a brand-new church called Mount Zion.

I looked at Cora. She opened her book and started reading again. Daddy was always talking about how great Greenwood was. He loved to tell us about how Negroes had settled here and built it from the ground up into the richest, most successful Black community in the country.

Cora never seemed interested. She was sixteen, four years older than me, and her mind was on two things: getting into Tuskegee and getting out of Greenwood. Going to college in Alabama gave her the perfect reason.

Daddy went on. "Greenwood has its own spirit," he said. "It's in the town, but it lives inside the people. You know people have actually *walked* to

Greenwood from other states? That's how great it is!" he said.

Usually, I liked to listen to Daddy's stories about Greenwood, but not today. Today, I wanted to go to the parade.

Cora had told me all about it before we fell asleep last night. She had heard about it from a friend at school whose daddy was a landscaper in downtown Tulsa.

"They're selling silk poppies straight from France," Cora had said. "Hundreds of them. There's going to be a motorcycle escort and a seventy-piece marching band. And I heard some of the ladies in town are buying new spring dresses just for the parade."

I looked out the window again. There wasn't going to be any band marching down Greenwood Avenue. And Daddy's roses were pretty, but they sure weren't silk.

Daddy clapped his hands. "Tell you what. We can have our own little parade in our own downtown. We can march right on into Deep Greenwood and do a little window shopping. Maybe even get a treat."

"Oh, that's a good idea," said Mama.

Cora let out a deep breath and closed her book again. She didn't look excited.

I smiled at Daddy. *Better than nothing*, I thought.

Deep Greenwood
May 30, 1921
10:45 a.m.

By the time we got into Deep Greenwood, I was excited. I had even put on my pink Easter dress and shiny black shoes, since the people at the parade were dressing up. The whole time we walked, I imagined I was at the parade in downtown Tulsa.

It seemed silly to me that Daddy wouldn't take us there. It was just across the Frisco train tracks from Deep Greenwood.

How can a skinny line of tracks make such a big difference? I thought.

I stopped in front of a shop and elbowed Cora. "Look, Cora. Fur coats. One day I'm going to have a fur coat," I said.

Cora laughed. "One day, I'm going to have *two*. And I'll wear them both at the same time.*"

"You certainly could have two," Daddy said with a laugh. "In Greenwood, anything is possible."

We passed by the barbershop, and the barber waved at Daddy. He had been cutting Daddy's hair since Daddy was young. The barber yelled through the open door. "Hey, Calvin!"

Daddy grinned and waved back. "Hey, Mr. Wilson! I'll be in next week," he said.

Mr. Wilson looked too old to still be a barber, but he didn't act old. His wife had passed away last year, and now he lived by himself. He never seemed lonely, though.

Cora and I walked ahead of Mama and Daddy and stopped in front of the jewelry store window. Daddy had told me that this was where he had bought Mama's two rings. Her engagement ring was a gold band, and her wedding ring was a gold band with one diamond right in the middle.

"After I finish college and become a doctor," said Cora, "I'm going to come in here and buy some diamond earrings."

I looked at my sister. "I thought you said you were leaving Greenwood? You're going to come back just to buy earrings?"

"Nope. I'm coming back to visit you all *and* buy diamond earrings. Two pairs. One for you and one for me."

I didn't know any women who were doctors, but I knew Cora was smart enough to be one. She'd probably read all the doctor books in the library before she graduated from high school.

I wished she wanted to come back and be a doctor *here*. Greenwood would be even better with my sister, the doctor, in it.

Daddy said the people made Greenwood what it was. They were hardworking, dedicated, and smart.

My parents fit right in. Mama taught at Booker T. Washington High School, and Daddy was a lawyer. Even though I didn't know what I wanted to be when I grew up, I fit in too. I always got top marks in school.

Daddy came up behind us. "Want to stop at the bakery?" he asked. "Best jelly rolls in the world, right here in Greenwood!"

Cora and I nodded, and we headed toward the bakery. Farther down the street, a jazz band sat outside the club and played on the sidewalk.

We got our treats, and even though it was raining a little bit, we sat on a bench to listen.

Cora smiled, took a bite of jelly roll, and pulled her jacket tighter around her.

I watched a few people in raincoats walk in and out of the shops. A man and a woman walked past.

"Sure was strange," said the woman. "Dick Rowland running through here like his hair was on fire."

"Wonder where he was running to," the man said.

"Or running *from,*" said the woman.

I looked at Mama and Daddy. They were listening too. I didn't know who Dick Rowland was, but Daddy looked like he might.

"Daddy, what do you think happened?" I asked.

Mama answered, "Worry about yourself, Lena. It's probably just gossip. "

But Daddy looked worried. "Hopefully nothing," he said.

From the way he said it, I had a feeling it might be *something.*

CHAPTER **TWO**

After school let out, I walked to the corner of Greenwood Avenue and Haskell Street. A breeze carried the smell of barbeque from Deep Greenwood, and my stomach growled. Since Mama taught at Cora's school, we always met up on the corner and walked the rest of the way home together.

Halfway home, Cora was still talking about science class. "And this summer," she said, "some of the high school students can apply to be interns with nurses in town."

"That sounds like a wonderful opportunity, Cora," said Mama. "And how was your day, Lena?"

I didn't hear Mama's question because I was watching a little group of people standing outside of someone's house. Two women and a man were whispering about something. The man was holding a newspaper.

"Lena?" said Mama, louder this time.

"Huh?" I asked.

"You mean, *yes?* How was your day at school?" she repeated.

"It was fine," I said. "Mama, why do you think those people are whispering like that?"

Mama and Cora both glanced in the direction I was looking. "Who knows?" said Mama.

Then I noticed four men farther down the street. They were huddled together whispering too.

"I think something's going on," I said.

I remembered yesterday in Deep Greenwood, when I'd overheard about the man running through town. Mama had said it was probably gossip. I had almost forgotten about it, but now, with all the whispering, it came back to me. The look on Daddy's face came back to me too.

Mama didn't answer me. She had spotted the men too. Even Cora looked curious about the whispering.

As we got closer, I saw that one of the men had a copy of the *The Tulsa Tribune* tucked under his arm. *The Tulsa Tribune* was the white newspaper. Greenwood had its own, *The Tulsa Star*. That was the one Daddy always read.

"Mama," I whispered, "why do they have the white newspaper instead of ours? Do you think that's what they're talking about?"

"Shhh," said Mama. "We are certainly not going to add to the whispering."

I studied Mama's face. There was just a little bit of worry in between her eyebrows. It was enough to keep me quiet for the rest of the walk.

When we got home, Mama went into the kitchen to get dinner started. Cora and I sat in the living room to do our homework. We didn't do our homework, though. We peeked out the window and whispered, just like the rest of Greenwood seemed to be doing. Over the next half hour, more people grouped together up and down the street.

"What do you think they're talking about?" I whispered to Cora.

She shook her head. "I don't know," she whispered back. "Nothing ever happens here."

Hopefully nothing, I thought, remembering Daddy's words.

"Cora, do you think it's about the man who ran through town yesterday?" I asked.

My sister's eyes got big. "I don't know. Maybe."

Just then, Daddy came home and caught us at the window. "That homework's not going to do itself," he said. "Come on out of that window and get started."

He kissed us on our foreheads, and I noticed he had a rolled-up newspaper in his hand. I couldn't see much of it, but I made out the letters *bune*. Daddy had bought a copy of *The Tulsa Tribune* too. Something was definitely going on and it had to do with the newspaper—the white newspaper.

Daddy went into the kitchen, and I heard him and Mama whispering. I tried to eavesdrop, but they were too quiet. After a while, I heard the paper rustling, and then they were silent.

Are they reading something? I wondered.

Cora and I did our best to work on our lessons, but I couldn't focus. I only got one arithmetic problem done before Mama said, "Girls! Wash up for dinner!"

As soon as we were all at the table and the food was served, I asked, "Daddy, is something wrong?"

"No, I'm fine. Why?" he said.

"I mean is something wrong in Greenwood? Everybody's whispering and carrying around newspapers," I explained.

Daddy and Mama had a quick conversation with their eyes. He nodded at her, then took a deep breath.

"Well," said Daddy, "someone was arrested."

"Someone from Greenwood?" I asked.

Cora put down her fork, and Mama picked up her water glass and took a sip. I waited.

"Yes," said Daddy. "Dick Rowland was accused of assaulting a white woman in the Drexel Building in downtown Tulsa."

Dick Rowland. That was the name I'd heard yesterday. Dick Rowland had run through town like his hair was on fire.

Does that mean he's guilty? Was he running from the police? I wondered.

Daddy took another deep breath and went on. "There are rumors that the white people of Tulsa want to lynch him."

The rice and gravy I had just put in my mouth stuck in my throat. You didn't have to leave Greenwood to know what lynching meant. Lynching meant hanging.

"But, Daddy," I said, "what if he didn't do it?"

Mama put down her glass. "It might not matter." Her voice was quiet. "The accusation is enough for some people."

"That boy didn't hurt anybody," said Daddy.

"You know him?" I asked. "He's a boy?"

"I know him a little bit," said Daddy. "He's nineteen. Mr. Wilson cuts his hair. I'm glad he's already caught though, guilty or not. He might be safer in jail than he is out."

"I don't know," said Mama. "If people in Greenwood are whispering about white folks storming the jail, a lynching might be exactly what happens."

I looked at Cora. She looked at her food but didn't eat any of it.

Daddy balled his napkin up in his fist. "All we are to them is the help," he said between his teeth. "That's why I'll never work downtown. They want us to mow their lawns and tend to their children and houses and shine their shoes. But the minute one of us is accused of something, they turn on us."

Mama put a hand on Daddy's arm. Her voice was soft. "Maybe Dick will be okay. Maybe they won't get to him. Maybe it's just a rumor."

"White vigilantes lynched one of their own last year," said Daddy. "They'll certainly lynch one of us."

I didn't know what a vigilante was, but it wasn't the time to ask. I stayed quiet so they'd keep talking.

"Calvin," said Mama. She waited until Daddy looked at her, then flicked her eyes at us. She didn't want us to hear this.

"Pearl, they have to know," he said. "Greenwood has kept them safe, but they have to know what the world is like."

Cora frowned. Daddy had been warning her about racism in the world outside of Greenwood ever since she mentioned going to Tuskegee.

The kitchen was completely silent except for the clock on the wall ticking. Finally, Daddy mumbled, "Nothing ever changes."

"Girls, go finish your homework," said Mama. She stood behind Daddy and put her hands on his shoulders.

Daddy looked like he wanted to punch a hole in the wall . . . or cry. Maybe both.

Cora and I got up and out of the kitchen as fast as possible. I didn't think either one of us wanted to hear any more.

Greenwood, Oklahoma
May 31, 1921
9:30 p.m.

Cora and I were still in the living room, trying to do our homework, when someone knocked on our front door. We both jumped.

Daddy rushed in from the kitchen where he was still whispering with Mama to answer it. Mama stood in the doorway to the kitchen, waiting to see who it was.

Mr. Wilson, the barber, stood on our doorstep. He was holding a rifle. "Calvin," he said, "we need you."

Everyone in my family sucked in a breath. It felt like we held all the air from the room in our lungs.

"Mr. Wilson, what's going on?" asked Daddy.

"A mob of white Tulsans is gathering outside of the courthouse where they're holding Dick Rowland," said Mr. Wilson. "Some of the men went down there to offer protection, but the sheriff told them it's 'under control.' Ain't nothing about this situation *under control*."

"So what's happening now?" asked Daddy.

Mr. Wilson had a serious look on his face. "We need to protect our own."

Daddy nodded.

"Daddy, please stay here," said Cora.

Mama said, "Calvin, you know this is going to mean a confrontation."

"We need you," said Mr. Wilson again.

I walked to the door and stood next to Daddy. He looked down at me with sad eyes, and I knew we were thinking the same thing. Helping the men of Greenwood was the right thing to do, but it was also dangerous.

I tried to keep the worry out of my voice. "You have to go, Daddy," I said.

Daddy put his hand on the top of my head. It felt heavy. He stared at me for a long time, then nodded.

Without a word, Daddy grabbed his jacket and hat off the coatrack. He stepped onto the front porch. Before he shut the door, he looked back at us.

"Lock the door, Pearl. I love you all," he said. And then he closed the door behind himself.

Cora ran to Mama, and they hugged and cried. Watching them, I suddenly realized helping was more than just dangerous. Daddy was walking right into what could be Dick Rowland's death *and* his own.

We stared at the door for what felt like a long time after Daddy left. Finally, Mama said, "Go on and finish your work. It's getting late." Then she disappeared into the kitchen.

I tried to get my work done, but I couldn't stop thinking about Daddy. Cora pretended she was reading, but her eyes stayed on the same spot on the page. Mama came back and sat on the sofa with her knitting and a cup of tea. I could tell she was trying to act like nothing was wrong.

But our pretending ended when a faraway *bang!* interrupted it.

Cora looked at me, and I looked at Mama. Mama put her teacup down too hard, and it made a big clanging noise. We waited in silence, but not for long. Another *bang!* echoed from outside.

This time I knew for sure what it was—gunfire. And I had a feeling it was coming from downtown Tulsa—where Daddy was.

CHAPTER **THREE**

Cora and I sat on each side of Mama, and she took our hands. "Dear Lord," she whispered, "please keep Calvin safe. Keep them all safe."

We sat like that, listening to shots in the night, and worrying and praying for almost an hour. Finally Mama said, "Lena, I want you to go to bed, okay?"

"What about Cora?" I asked. I didn't want to be in our bedroom without Cora. Not on this night.

"Lena, *please* just go get in bed," Mama said. "Try to get some sleep. You have school tomorrow."

I did what Mama said, but I didn't fall asleep. I wanted to see Daddy walk back through the front door. I wanted to know right away that he was okay. I didn't want to wait until the morning. I needed to know that doing the right thing didn't kill my daddy.

I lay on my back and pulled the covers up to my chin. It seemed like the guns would never stop. It also seemed like they were getting closer.

I repeated Mama's prayer in my head. *Dear Lord, please keep Daddy safe. Keep them all safe.*

I stayed in bed until I couldn't stand it anymore. Then I tiptoed down the hall and peeked into the living room. Mama and Cora were still sitting together on the sofa.

Before I could say anything, a thumping came from the porch. All three of us jumped, then froze.

The sound came again, sort of a thumping and scraping sound at the front door. Mama jumped up and grabbed Cora, and I ran to them.

Mama dragged us away from the door and shoved us behind her. I wasn't sure what—or who—she thought might be out there, but my heart was pounding.

The doorknob jiggled. Then there was a rummaging sound, followed by a light knock. I could feel Mama shaking.

There was another knock at the door. This time it was harder.

"Pearl?" It was Daddy's voice. "It's me."

Mama didn't move. It was like she didn't recognize Daddy's voice. He knocked again and called her name. This time, Mama ran to the door and swung it open.

Daddy stood on the other side. His hat was squished, and his jacket was wrinkled. I looked for scratches or bruises or blood, but I didn't see any.

The next thing I knew, the three of us had Daddy trapped in the doorway, wrapped up in all

six of our arms. He pushed into the house with us surrounding him, then closed and locked the door.

"Thank God," cried Mama.

"Downtown Tulsa is a battleground," said Daddy. He sat in the armchair, looking as relieved to be home as we were to have him there.

"There was a scuffle between one of us and one of them, and a gun went off. It went south fast after that," he continued. "Men got hit by stray bullets. Somebody said they saw the sheriff run and hide in the hotel. Seems like the shooting went on for almost two hours. At least a dozen men were killed, colored and white."

"How did you get away?" Cora asked.

"It wasn't easy," said Daddy. "The shooting spread toward the Frisco tracks."

I was right. The gunshots *were* getting closer. I was glad they had stayed on the white side of the tracks.

Daddy went on. "The white people looted Bardon's Sporting Goods to get guns. And the police were right there with them, Pearl. They're even deputizing folks."

"What's deputizing?" I asked, but nobody answered.

"The police were looting the store with the mob?" asked Cora.

Daddy didn't answer us, but the answers were on his face. The Tulsa police were not there to protect us. They were ready to kill us, just like the rest of them.

We stared at Daddy and waited for him to finish. When he talked again, he sounded tired.

"We were outnumbered. There were hundreds of white people in that mob." He shook his head like he couldn't believe it himself. "Not everyone got out."

"Did they get Dick Rowland, Daddy?" I asked.

"Not yet," said Daddy. "The sheriff had him on the top floor of the courthouse. They disabled the elevator and had deputies guarding the stairs."

"Did Mr. Wilson make it out?" asked Mama.

Daddy nodded. "That's one tough old man."

"I'm glad you came back instead of trying to fight all those people," said Cora.

Daddy stood up and hugged her. "You all look tired," he said. "We all have to get up in the morning, so let's get you to bed."

First, Daddy tucked Mama into bed like she was a little girl. Then he walked us to our room. Cora seemed happy to climb in bed, but I wanted to talk some more.

"Daddy, can I get some water first?" I asked.

We tiptoed out of the room so Cora could sleep. "Let's have some warm milk," said Daddy.

I sat at the table, and Daddy poured some milk into a boiler. Then he put a little bit of honey in and heated it up. When it was ready, he brought two mugs to the table and sat down. In the distance, I could still hear gunshots.

At least Daddy is home, I thought. I knew his trip into downtown Tulsa could have gone much worse.

"What will happen now?" I asked.

"Well, hopefully they'll go home, and that will be the end of it," he said. "Don't you worry."

But Daddy's face was full of just that—worry. He didn't think that was the end of it. I could tell.

The worry was catching too. I felt like I had maggots squirming in my stomach. I pushed my milk away.

"It's after midnight," said Daddy. "You need to get in bed."

Daddy picked me up like I only weighed two pounds and carried me to bed. He fixed my covers for me and tucked them in all the way around. Cora was already asleep.

"Daddy?" I whispered. "Can you leave the door cracked?"

He nodded and headed to the door.

"And the hall light on?" I asked.

Daddy nodded again, then left the room.

Laying in the quiet, tucked in so tight I couldn't move, I stared at the strip of light on the ceiling and listened to the gunshots. I tried not to worry, but the harder I tried, the more worried I got.

I only knew I fell asleep because something woke me up all of a sudden.

Bang! Bang!

The noise outside was *loud*—much louder than before. It sounded like it was right outside of our window.

I looked across our bedroom. Cora sat straight up in bed.

"I think somebody's shooting at our house!" I screamed.

CHAPTER FOUR

The sound came again. *Bang! Bang!*

Cora and I jumped out of bed and ran to the hall. Mama and Daddy were already on their way to our room.

"Daddy, somebody's shooting out there!" I yelled.

"Who is it?" asked Cora. "What should we do?"

I stared at Mama and Daddy. They were dressed and had their coats on. Mama held her purse. They looked at each other.

Before our parents could answer us, there was a long, loud whistle from outside. I couldn't tell if it was from a train on the Frisco tracks or a factory in Tulsa. After the whistle stopped, the shooting got worse.

Bang! Bang! Bang!

People outside shouted. It sounded like half the neighborhood was out there.

"Put on your coats and shoes," said Daddy. "Hurry up."

The gunshots were firing one after the other, so we did what Daddy said, even though we still had on our nightgowns. While we were in our room getting our shoes, Cora threw a few things in her own bag. I couldn't tell what in the dark, though.

When we were finished, Daddy grabbed each of our hands and pulled us through the hall to the kitchen. He turned the table on its side and pushed us to the floor behind it, then crouched down behind us.

"Daddy, what's happening?" I yelled. I hoped the table would protect us from the bullets if they came through the windows or walls.

"Shhh," said Mama. "Some of the folks from downtown made their way into Greenwood. Just stay quiet."

Mama put her arm around me, and I felt her body trembling.

I didn't know what a war was like, but to me it sounded like there was one happening right in front of our house. It got louder and louder outside.

When the phone rang, we all jumped.

Daddy motioned for us to stay behind the table. He crawled over to the phone and picked it up. "Hello? Mr. Wilson . . . what? . . . okay." Then he hung up and crawled back.

"What is it, Calvin?" whispered Mama.

Daddy took a deep breath. "Mr. Wilson's making a run for it. Said it looks like the mob has more than doubled since we were downtown. They're running wild through Deep Greenwood."

Mama and Daddy had another eyeball conversation, but this time Mama's eyes were filled with tears. "Calvin, we can't stay here."

"Mama, I don't want to go outside," said Cora.

"Me neither," I said. *There are people ready to kill us outside.*

Daddy sat on the floor facing us. "Listen, we have to get out of here while we can. These people don't know when to stop."

"We have to stick together," said Mama. "Hold hands, and don't let go. No matter what."

"Stay low," said Daddy. "And keep your eyes open. It sounds like bullets are flying in all directions."

Bang! Bang!

Bang!

Bang! Bang! Bang!

The noise outside sounded even worse now that I knew we were about to go out there. Next to me, Cora started to cry. Mama grabbed her hand, and Daddy grabbed mine. We all crept to the front door on our knees.

Daddy opened the door a little bit and looked out. He turned to us and said, "It's a mess out there. Stay close."

We all got to our feet and hunched over. The air drifting in through the crack in the door smelled like smoke. The yelling and shooting seemed like it was coming from everywhere.

Daddy squeezed my hand and pulled me with him as he dashed to the sidewalk.

Greenwood didn't even look like Greenwood anymore. Our terrified neighbors were scattered in the street. There were old people in nightclothes trying to walk fast. Mamas with little babies tucked into their robes raced down the street. Whole families were holding hands and running in a line. One lady wore a nightgown and a fur coat.

Some people looked like they had run out of the house without even thinking. They had no coats and no shoes. Most of them were going toward the Midland Valley train tracks on the east side of town. A few of them were getting into their cars.

"Daddy," I said, "where should we go?"

"Maybe we can get to Mount Zion," he said. "Hide in the basement."

We all nodded and started running in the direction of the church. It was the opposite direction from where everyone else was going, but Daddy's idea was a good one. Mount Zion was one of the newest buildings in Greenwood. That meant it was probably one of the strongest.

We had only gone a block when a car turned onto our street. It headed straight toward us. The

headlights blinded me, but I could still see what was poking out of the windows.

Shotguns.

Daddy dived behind somebody's rosebushes, pulling me with him. Mama and Cora crashed into us. Cora sucked in air, and I knew she had scratched herself on the thorns. None of us made a sound.

Through the bushes, I saw a truck with white men in it. The one in the passenger seat leaned out the open window.

Bang! Bang!

Gunshots and screams and smoke filled the air. All I could do was cover my face with my hands and pray nobody had been hit. The men in the truck whooped and hollered, and the driver stepped on the gas.

I peeked through the bushes again. "Daddy," I said, "that truck came from the direction of Mount

Zion. Everyone is going away from the church. Maybe we should too."

"I think we should go back home and hide in the house," said Cora.

Mama said, "Calvin, we need a plan."

"Shhh," said Daddy. "Let me think."

Daddy wasn't too sure about his plan anymore. I could tell.

The maggots in my stomach started squirming again. I looked toward Deep Greenwood and saw smoke rising. Flames reached for the sky. The sky was glowing a few blocks away above Archer Street too.

Greenwood is burning, I realized.

BangBangBangBangBang!

In the street, someone yelled, "They're at Standpipe Hill firing a machine gun at the church! There's another one at Sunset Hill. Our snipers don't have a chance!"

"Daddy, we have to get out of here!" I said.

"Follow me!" yelled Daddy.

All four of us held hands—Daddy, then me, then Cora, then Mama. Daddy ran like I'd never seen him run before. This time, he headed away from the church, dragging us along behind him.

I didn't know what we were running toward. I only knew what we were running from. *Death.*

CHAPTER **FIVE**

Greenwood, Oklahoma
June 1, 1921
5:45 a.m.

I ran as fast as I could. It seemed like almost everyone on our end of Greenwood was headed in the same direction now—away from the church.

A few white men on foot had made it to our neighborhood. They had guns, but so did some of the Greenwood men. Bullets flew, and people dodged them. Every time one hit the street, there was a shattering sound and a spark.

Daddy pulled us closer to the houses. I stayed close, but I knew houses wouldn't save us if a bullet came our way.

I tried not to look at the street. I didn't want to see what was happening, but it was impossible to ignore. Even through my tears, I could see men and women lying dead in the streets.

Some of the Greenwood men stood like lonely guards in front of their homes. They held shotguns that wouldn't save them or their houses.

We crossed Greenwood Avenue. It looked like the entire street was on fire. White men with oil cans and torches were setting fire to everything in sight. Some of the Greenwood business owners were trying to fight back, but there were too many invaders.

Some of the white people wore regular clothes, but some wore uniforms.

This is what Daddy was talking about earlier, I realized. *The police and home guards are helping the mob. They don't care about us at all.*

The sweat between my hand and Daddy's made my hand come loose from his, and I tripped.

"Lena!" yelled Daddy. "Come on, baby. We have to keep going."

Daddy and Cora helped me up. We took hands again, and Daddy paused. He took my face in his hands, wiped away my tears, and kissed my forehead.

"I know," he whispered.

"Girls, don't look," said Mama. She and Cora were crying too.

We grabbed hands, and Daddy started running again. I focused on the back of his jacket. My heart pounded louder than the gunshots and screams.

Don't look. Don't look, I repeated to myself.

On the next block, white men and women were stealing from empty houses. Men ran in and came out with Victrolas and furniture. Women left wearing jewelry and furs. They yelled and laughed while they destroyed or stole everything that was ours.

We never did anything to them, I thought. *Why are they doing this to us?*

"Jesus," Daddy whispered.

I peeked around him to see what he was looking at. A block away, two rows of Greenwood men were being led away at gunpoint by white men. I didn't want to know where they were being taken.

Daddy dragged us to the left and into someone's backyard. We kneeled next to a chicken coop, and Mama and Cora sobbed. Daddy dabbed at his forehead with his sleeve.

I wiped my eyes and took deep breaths. I knew pretty soon we would be running again.

At the far end of the yard, several people from Greenwood huddled behind a tree. I tugged on Daddy's coat and pointed toward them.

He nodded. "We need to find a place to hide."

"I don't think we can stay in Greenwood," said Mama. "It's not safe anywhere."

Daddy didn't answer. He stared at the smoky, glowing sky, deep in thought.

My eyes searched for an answer, and that's when I noticed eyes staring at me from inside the chicken coop. They weren't chicken eyes—they were human. And I recognized them.

"Mr. Wilson?" I whispered.

He put his finger to his lips. My whole family looked at me, then at the chicken coop.

"Mr. Wilson?" said Daddy. "What are you doing in there?"

"I'm hit," said Mr. Wilson.

"Hit where?" Daddy asked.

"My leg," said Mr. Wilson. "Stray bullet got me. I can't make it out."

"Where were you headed?" asked Mama. I could tell from her voice that she hoped Mr. Wilson knew of somewhere we could go.

"North," he said. "A bunch of folks are headed into the country. Some are following the Midland Valley Tracks. Trying to hide in the woods."

Two thoughts came into my mind at the same time. *We need to go north like everyone else. And we have to take Mr. Wilson with us.*

"Cora," I said, "can you help him?"

Mama and Daddy helped Mr. Wilson out of the coop, and we all squatted behind it for cover. Mr. Wilson rolled up the leg of his pants so Cora could see his wound.

"Looks like the bullet grazed the side of your leg," Cora said. "Mama, can I have your scarf?"

Mama handed her scarf to Cora, who wrapped it around Mr. Wilson's leg.

While Cora tended to Mr. Wilson, I looked up at the sky. The sun was just starting to come up, so it looked pink and gray. It was like even the sun couldn't bear to look, so it was hiding behind the smoke.

Maybe the mob will go away when the sun comes up, I thought.

As soon as I thought it, my hope disappeared. A plane came from somewhere past the tracks and swooped down over Greenwood. It was so low I could see the pilot.

"Daddy!" screamed Cora. "Are those war planes?"

Between the roar of the plane and the blasts of gunshots I felt like a soldier in a war. I knew one thing about war—it left a lot of people dead. Whatever kind of planes they were, they weren't there to help my people any more than the police and home guards were.

The plane traveled farther across Greenwood, and something dropped from it. There was an explosion when it hit the ground.

"Daddy are they dropping bombs on us?" I screamed.

"We need to get north!" Daddy yelled above the chaos filling the air. "*Now!*"

My family stood up and took hands again. Mr. Wilson thanked Cora, then made his way back to the coop.

"Mr. Wilson," I said, "you're coming with us."

He looked down at his leg and shook his head.

"We'll help you," I said, looking at Mama and Daddy.

Mama nodded, and Daddy said, "Lena is right. Let's go, Mr. Wilson. You're coming with us."

Cora and I let go of each other's hands and let Mr. Wilson get in the middle. Tears filled his eyes, and he took our hands.

As dawn broke, Daddy led us through the crowd of our fleeing neighbors. I looked back toward Deep Greenwood. It looked like a dying, fire-breathing dragon.

I wondered if it would be there when we got back.

CHAPTER SIX

The rising sun was a blessing and a curse. We could see better, but that meant we could see more of the loss and destruction. More people lay in the streets than before. It seemed like every building in Greenwood was on fire.

I thought back to Memorial Day and eating jelly rolls on the bench with Cora. I remembered how we dreamed of diamonds and fur coats. In my mind, I could still see Daddy grinning and waving at Mr. Wilson, who was now limping along with my family.

Yesterday felt like a year ago. All of the sad feelings in my heart turned into anger.

Greenwood was *ours*. Even if Dick Rowland had attacked that lady, we didn't deserve this.

Another plane roared toward us. All around us, neighbors scattered and looked for places to hide.

"This way!" yelled Daddy.

He tugged on my arm, and we all shuffled as fast as we could around a corner and behind a fence. A man and his pregnant wife ducked behind the fence with us.

BangBangBangBang! Bullets flew, and the plane swooped.

It seemed like there was a never-ending supply of bullets. I couldn't even tell if they were coming from the sky or the ground.

A chorus of screams and yells rose from the other side of the fence, and my anger rose with it.

I peeked through a hole in the fence. A truckload of white men with guns turned south, leaving our fallen men and women behind them. Another group of our men was being marched west at gunpoint.

"Daddy, look," I said. I moved out of the way so he could see through the hole. "Where are they taking them?"

"I don't know," he said. "Probably nowhere good."

The man next to us said, "They're herding as many of us as they can into Convention Hall. Said they're *protecting* us." He made a laughing sound that wasn't really a laugh.

Daddy looked at Mr. Wilson. "Maybe it would be easier to get us all to Convention Hall. It could be safer there than out in the open. Especially in the daylight."

"Maybe they can bandage up your leg," I chimed in.

Then I looked at the spot of blood at the bottom of Cora's nightgown. I knew it was from when we hid behind the rosebushes.

"Maybe they can clean up your leg too, Cora," I added.

Mr. Wilson shook his head. "I'm not going to no Convention Hall to be caged like an animal. I don't trust them for one minute. I'll walk north 'til I can't walk anymore."

"I don't trust them either then," I whispered to Cora. "We have to take care of ourselves."

"And each other," said Cora quietly.

There was a moment of silence, but it was interrupted by bullets hitting the other side of the fence. We all ducked and huddled together on the ground. The pregnant lady hugged her stomach while her husband used his own body as a shield.

When the bullets stopped, Daddy stood up. I could tell he had made up his mind.

"We'll keep north. Let's go," he said.

Mr. Wilson nodded. The other man got up and helped his wife up. Then he and Daddy helped Mr. Wilson to his feet.

Daddy and the man made eye contact, and the man nodded and said, "Byron."

"Calvin," Daddy replied. Then he pointed to each of us and said our names.

Byron was about to say his wife's name when gunshots echoed in the morning air. They were so close I could feel the sound in my body.

"We can't wait any longer," said Daddy.

More bullets hit the fence, and we didn't even take hands this time. We all ran with Daddy in the lead.

With bullets hitting the street only a few feet from us, we turned left and headed toward the rolling hills and woods. I hoped they would keep us alive.

CHAPTER **SEVEN**

The route north was full of people from
Greenwood. It was the opposite of everything
I imagined downtown Tulsa's Memorial Day
parade was.

There was no marching band playing. We walked
to the sounds of gunfire, our own sobs, and a baby
crying. Costumes and Sunday bests were replaced
by nightclothes, wrinkled suits, and stained dresses.

We didn't have a planned route. Nobody seemed
to have any idea where we were going. We just
kept north through the tall, dry grass. Ruts from

car wheels were the only clue we were going somewhere other people had gone before.

We were raggedy and dirty and exhausted. But more than anything, we were heartbroken.

As we walked, I thought about a funeral we had gone to for one of the elders of Greenwood a while back. Mama had called the walk to the cemetery "a funeral procession."

It felt a lot like this walk.

The higher the sun rose in the sky, the heavier my legs felt. Half of me wanted to stop and rest, but the other half wanted to get as far away from the mob as I could. Even though we traveled farther and farther away, we could still hear gunshots and explosions from Greenwood.

"Daddy, will they follow us?" I asked.

"I don't know," he said. "I pray they don't."

As soon as the words were out of Daddy's mouth, we heard a car coming. Everyone walking hid behind whatever they could find. Some jumped behind bushes and shrubs. Some, including us, just laid down right in the tall grass.

The man driving stopped and called out, "Anyone want a ride?"

It was one of our own. A family had managed to get out of Greenwood in their car. We all came out of hiding.

"Where to?" shouted a man holding a little girl's hand.

"Anywhere that's not here," the driver answered.

The man, his daughter, and his wife climbed into the back seat. Two ladies squished in with them, and off they went. The rest of us stared in silence as they disappeared.

A few more Greenwood cars went by, but they were already full. The people inside looked at us with serious faces and sad eyes. They nodded their well wishes and sorrows at us, and we nodded back.

I took Cora's hand, and we walked like that for a long time. As the day got warmer, the trip got harder. I felt like I had a throat full of fire and ashes. I could taste Greenwood in every breath.

Around us, some of the travelers whispered. Others cried. Mama and Daddy held hands in front of Cora and me.

Mr. Wilson lagged behind. Byron and his wife were farther back behind him.

"Y'all okay back there?" asked Mr. Wilson.

"We'll make it," answered Byron.

Up ahead, a baby started screaming. His mama moved him from one hip to the other.

One of the other women walked over and said something. The mama smiled and nodded, and the other woman took the baby. She gave him a cracker to chew on, and they walked along in silence.

I heard a thump behind me. I turned around to see Mr. Wilson on the ground.

Daddy ran back and helped him to his feet. A man we didn't even know hurried to help too. He got on one side of Mr. Wilson, and Daddy got on the other. They put Mr. Wilson's arms on their shoulders and their own arms around his waist. They half-walked, half-carried him up the path.

"It's not dead," I said to Cora.

She looked at me and frowned. "What isn't dead?" she asked.

"Greenwood," I said. "They can burn it down, but they can't take what built it out of us."

"What do you mean?" she asked.

"You know how Daddy is always talking about how much he loves Greenwood?" I said.

Cora nodded. She didn't make a face like she usually did when Daddy talked about how great Greenwood was.

"It's because Greenwood has its own spirit,"
I said. "It's in the town, but it lives inside the people, just like Daddy says. Look around."

Cora looked at our neighbors. Her eyes rested on the woman helping with the baby. Then she watched the stranger helping Mr. Wilson.

As far up the trail as we could see, people were helping each other. They carried each other's bags, helped each other take off coats, and shared any food they had managed to grab.

"They'll never take who we are away," I said. "They can't."

Cora nodded, and I felt like I had just a tiny bit more energy than I did before.

Once we were about two hours from Greenwood, some of us stopped to rest. Cora and I peeled off our jackets and put them on the ground to sit. The adults sat nearby and talked in low voices. Byron's wife laid down on his coat and put her head on his lap.

There was a house not too far away, and some people glanced at it out of the corner of their eyes. I could tell they were worried about what kind of person lived there. I was worried too. But we took a chance to catch our breath anyway.

I was the first one to see the door to the house swing open. A white man and woman came out on the porch.

"Hey!" the man hollered. "You all want to rest here?"

I wondered if it was a trick. I'd heard enough stories to know that plenty of white people didn't like us. And now I had seen with my own eyes just how true that was.

A murmur went through the people of Greenwood. Finally someone yelled, "I sure am thirsty. Can I trouble you for some water?"

The woman on the porch nodded and ran back in the house. She came back out with a bucket of water. A handful of people headed in their direction. The rest of us watched.

"Come on!" the man shouted and waved his arm. "You can rest out back under the trees."

"We'll share what we have," added the woman.

A few more of our neighbors slowly approached the house. We waited to see what would happen.

"I wouldn't trust them for a minute," said Byron. "They might take us out back and shoot us dead."

"I don't know about that," said Daddy. "But I don't have any reason to trust them either."

"Mmm-mmm," said Mr. Wilson. "Me neither."

Mama looked from one man to the other. Finally she whispered, "Calvin, those people seem okay. Maybe we can at least get some water. I know the girls are thirsty. I am too."

Daddy didn't answer her. Instead, we watched as more and more people wandered toward the porch. They scooped water from the bucket, and I could

almost feel it sliding, cool and smooth, down my own throat.

The woman handed out something else too, and people were eating it. From where I sat, it looked like bread.

The man on the porch directed the crowd around the side of the house. The people of Greenwood nodded and waved their thanks, and the woman grinned and nodded back. They seemed happy to help.

"Daddy," I said, "can we please just get water and then come back here?"

"No," said Daddy. "And that's that."

I looked around. We weren't the only ones who stayed put, but most of the group had accepted help. I didn't think those white people were going to hurt us. They probably felt sorry for us. Or maybe they were just nice. But I knew better than to talk back to Daddy.

I scooted closer to Cora and put my head on her shoulder. We watched the black smoke rise from Greenwood. Every now and then there was an explosion, and we both jumped.

Mama came and sat on our coats with us. I laid on her lap, and she rubbed my hair. My eyelids got heavy, but every time my eyes closed another explosion made them pop open again.

I couldn't relax. Not only were we hungry and thirsty, but we were out here in the open for anybody to come and find. And we couldn't sit here forever.

CHAPTER EIGHT

The rumbling of an engine woke me up. It took my brain a minute to catch up with my ears, but finally, it shouted at me. *Someone's coming!*

I sat up and scooted behind Mama. Cora moved closer too.

"It's the Red Cross!" yelled someone sitting farther down the path.

Some of the men stood up and watched the truck approach. As it got closer, I could see the red plus sign that stood for Red Cross. Help we could trust had finally come.

Daddy didn't budge. Mama was about to stand up, but he said, "Pearl, best to stay here."

"Calvin, it's the Red Cross," said Mama. "They aren't going to hurt us." She didn't get up though.

Daddy shook his head. "Doesn't matter who they say they are. *Home guards* invaded our homes."

"We need help," said Mama. "The kids are tired and hungry. We're out here in the open like sitting ducks."

"I'd rather be a sitting duck than a fool," said Daddy.

Cora started to cry, and Mama glared at Daddy. Words I couldn't quite hear rode on her breath and got lost in the air.

I frowned. I didn't want my parents to argue. I also didn't want to sit in the grass all day or keep walking toward nothing.

I watched as the Red Cross truck stopped next to a cluster of people. A man in the truck leaned out and said, "We're taking people down to First Presbyterian Church."

An older couple got in the truck right away. A few others slowly joined them.

I got up and squatted down next to Daddy. "Can we please go with them?"

He stared straight ahead with his jaw clenched so tight I could see it twitching under his skin. "Lena, we can't trust anybody but ourselves," he said.

"But, Daddy, aren't the Red Cross people the ones who go around helping people? Don't they feed people?" I asked.

"We don't need their help or their food," he said. "Plus, First Presbyterian is a white church in downtown Tulsa. That's the *last* place I want to be."

I looked at Mr. Wilson. Surely he wanted to leave with the Red Cross. He'd been walking on a shot leg for hours.

It was like he knew what I was thinking. He shook his head and said, "I'll stay here with you all."

"Us too," said Byron.

I looked at Mama. She patted the coat next to her so I'd come sit back down. I sat with my back to Daddy so I wouldn't get in trouble for glaring at him. We watched the truck fill up and finally drive back toward Tulsa. People who couldn't fit stood in the middle of the path and watched it disappear.

Next to me, Cora wiped her tears, opened her bag, and took out a book. I should have known that's what she was grabbing in the dark before we left.

"Will you read to me?" I asked Cora.

She smiled and read out loud. The book was about different sicknesses, and even though it was boring, the sound of Cora's voice helped me relax.

I don't know how much time passed, but it was long enough that Cora's voice started to sound hoarse. Eventually, we heard another engine coming.

It turned out to be the same truck with the same Red Cross people in it. They had come back for those who hadn't fit the first time.

Mama stood up and looked down at Daddy. "We need to go with them this time," she said softly. I had a feeling she was going no matter what Daddy thought.

Mr. Wilson struggled to his feet. "We can't stay here forever," he agreed. "My leg is throbbing. I don't want it to get infected."

Byron looked at his wife. "Baby, what do you want to do?" he asked.

"I have to eat something," she said. Then she started to cry. "And my stomach is cramping."

I don't know if Daddy felt outnumbered or if he knew he was wrong, but he stood up too. "All right," was all he said.

Without another word, Daddy helped Mr. Wilson onto the back of the truck. Then the rest of us climbed in. The back of the truck filled with more people than it could actually fit, and when it couldn't take another soul, we turned around and headed back toward Greenwood.

My heart pounded as we got closer and closer to home. Every now and then we'd hear gunshots or an explosion. Before long, we could see part of our town—or what was left of it.

The maggots in my stomach started up again as the truck dropped down the eastern border of Greenwood. Firefighters tried to put out fires, but it didn't matter. The houses were too far gone. Almost every building as far as I could see was destroyed. Some sections were nothing but gray rubble and smoke.

I didn't want to know what the rest of Greenwood looked like.

I looked at Daddy, and his eyes were full of tears. One fell before he could catch it, and he looked away.

There were a few white people walking among the destruction. I couldn't tell if they were helping or finishing the job they'd started. Some stared at us as we passed by. Some looked sad. Others sneered, and I wondered what crimes against my people they had committed.

And that's when I noticed the bodies in the street.

Mama noticed it at the same time and gasped. It felt like everything I had been holding inside burst out.

"Why did they do this to us?" I screamed. "They didn't have to *kill* us!"

Mama grabbed me and buried my face in her chest. "Don't look, Lena," she cried.

I could hear other people on the truck crying, and a few cursed. I wiggled away from Mama as we passed through Greenwood, over the Frisco tracks, and into downtown Tulsa.

Suddenly I understood why Daddy hadn't wanted to come. We were in the middle of white Tulsa. White Tulsans had attacked us, and there was no reason to believe they wouldn't attack us again right now.

I held my breath and shrunk backward into the crowd of my neighbors in the truck. I had changed my mind about seeing downtown Tulsa.

Please don't let them hurt us, I prayed.

CHAPTER **NINE**

Downtown Tulsa, Oklahoma
First Presbyterian Church
June 1, 1921
3:00 p.m.

As we slid off the back of the truck and shuffled

into First Presbyterian Church, I thanked God for

keeping me safe. Inside, the church was full of

people from Greenwood.

Some huddled together against the walls. Others

sat on the floor and whispered. Kids slept in the

arms of adults who looked like they needed naps

too. A few covered their faces with their hands and

cried. A couple of people stared into space.

There weren't just people from Greenwood

inside the church, though. There were also white

people. I wasn't used to being around white people. After what had happened, I didn't think I wanted to be.

A white lady dressed like a nurse came up to us. She looked at the scarf Mama had tied around Mr. Wilson's leg. "Let's get your leg taken care of," she said to him.

Mr. Wilson didn't resist. He just concentrated on the floor and limped along behind her as she led him away.

A second white lady walked up to us. "Come with me," she said.

I looked at Daddy to see what he thought. I wasn't sure if I should trust her or not. But Daddy nodded, so we followed her.

First, the lady gave us water. Even Daddy looked grateful. Next, she offered us fresh clothes. They had piles of all kinds of clothes.

Where did all those clothes come from? I wondered.

Byron took a clean shirt and so did Daddy. I didn't want to wear someone else's clothes, though, so I was glad when Mama said, "No, thank you."

Next, we washed up and sat on some chairs in a corner. Red Cross people brought us each a plate of food—ham sandwiches and strawberries, plus more water. They smiled at us with their mouths, but their eyes looked sad and almost sorry.

I waited until they left us alone to eat. I didn't want them staring at me, and I didn't want to seem too grateful. Once they walked away, I scarfed down my food so fast it stuck in my throat.

After we ate, Cora pulled out her book again. Mama rested her head on Daddy's shoulder. I was glad they weren't mad at each other anymore.

I searched the room for people I knew. I noticed a few people I'd seen in Deep Greenwood and some teachers and kids from my school. I didn't see any of the kids from my class, though.

Where are my friends? I wondered. I watched the people and eavesdropped on some ladies a few feet away.

"Do you know where they took the men?" asked one.

"I heard they took them to Convention Hall and McNulty Park," said another.

"The fairgrounds too," a third lady said. "Only now they won't let them leave."

"Not my husband," whispered a woman with tears falling like raindrops on her chest. "They shot him right on our own porch. He was trying to protect me and our house."

The first woman said, "Then he died a hero, and don't you forget it." She sounded angry. "I live— *lived*—next door to an older couple. They decided to stay in their house." The woman took a deep breath. "Their house was invaded, and somebody shot them while they *prayed*."

A woman who had been quiet said, "They told A.C. Jackson they were protecting him. He cooperated . . . and they shot him for it."

Dr. Jackson? I thought.

Everybody knew Dr. Jackson. He was a famous surgeon—and not just in Greenwood. He was so good he even had *white* patients.

I had heard enough. I didn't need to hear all of the stories to know that what the white Tulsans had done to us was unforgivable.

A white man from the Red Cross appeared in the doorway. "The Salvation Army is hiring men to help bury the dead," he called out. "Any man willing to help, please step forward."

The ladies nearby started whispering again. "Our people deserve a proper funeral," said one.

The woman next to her said, "First they take our men and burn down our homes, then they ask *us* to bury them."

She shook her head like she couldn't believe it.

I thought back to the Greenwood men I'd seen being led away at gunpoint. *Please don't let them all be dead*, I prayed.

Daddy and Byron stood up right away. A few other men stood up too, but only a few. That's all there were.

Even though I knew we probably didn't have a single thing left to our names, Daddy stood tall and pushed his shoulders back. And I knew why. He always talked about our people—Black people—building Greenwood up from nothing.

"There's no place quite like Greenwood anywhere in the country," he always told me.

And it wasn't because of the buildings. It was because of the people.

And now my daddy was going to be one of those people who cleaned up Greenwood. He was going to hold his head up high and walk into the middle of all that destruction, and he was going to bury our friends and neighbors.

My mind tried to show me a picture of the people shot and burned in the streets, but I shut it out. It tried to remind me of the bullets flying through the air, of pregnant women running for their lives, of white men shooting at us from a truck.

But I wouldn't let it.

Instead, I thought of Daddy and Mr. Wilson heading into the night to protect Dick Rowland. I thought about the jazz band and the jewelry shop and jelly rolls.

I remembered the theater and the school and the library. I remembered Thursday evenings, when it seemed like all our neighbors paraded into Deep Greenwood to be happy and proud and feel good about being Black.

As Daddy walked toward the door of First Presbyterian Church, I ran after him and threw

my arms around him. He hugged me tight and whispered in my year, "We're going to be okay."

"Be careful, Daddy," I said.

I felt his head nod against my shoulder. "I will."

I watched the men of Greenwood form a small cluster near the door. They stood tall and ready. Ready to honor our dead. Ready to provide for their families. Ready to rebuild.

CHAPTER **TEN**

Tulsa, Oklahoma
First Presbyterian Church
June 3, 1921
5:00 p.m.

For days, Daddy dug graves at Oaklawn Cemetery in Tulsa. While he dug, Mama, Cora, Byron's wife—Daisy—and I got to know some of the other people staying in the church.

At first, people talked about the horrible things they'd seen the night of the massacre, but eventually they stopped. It was like talking about it kept it alive. Nobody wanted to relive it over and over again.

When Daddy came back to the church after his third day of working, he said, "I've helped dig well over one hundred graves. I need a break, and I think it's time for us to think about going back. A group of people is returning to Greenwood tomorrow. Some went back today."

Mama's eyes looked scared, and she shook her head. Cora and I looked at each other. We hadn't forgotten what we'd seen when we rode through Greenwood on our way to downtown Tulsa.

"Daddy, is there anywhere to go back to?" I asked.

Daddy took a deep breath and let it out. Then he leaned forward and looked me straight in the eye.

"I've heard talk," he said. "Greenwood is all but gone. It's going to be hard to look at."

"Is our house still there?" Cora asked.

"Probably not," Daddy said.

"Where will we stay?" asked Mama.

Daddy rubbed his face. "The men I've been working with have been planning their return," he said. "They want to pitch tents to stay in while we rebuild Greenwood."

Mama frowned the whole time Daddy talked. Some of the people sitting near us listened. Some of them nodded like they thought going home and getting to work was the best plan. Others shook their heads.

"I'll never, ever, ever go back to Greenwood," said one man.

I whispered to Cora, "I'm scared to go back. I don't want to see it."

"Me neither," she said. "I already wanted to leave Greenwood. Now I really don't want to live there."

"But it's home," I said.

"It *was* home," answered Cora.

Our group was quiet and nervous as we made our way through downtown Tulsa. Even though it was the same route some of our neighbors had walked every day to and from work, it wasn't the same.

As we approached the Frisco tracks, nobody in our group said a word. Mama, who stood between me and Cora, took our hands.

"Dear Lord," she whispered, "please help me through this."

All twenty or so of us stood and stared. Greenwood was completely destroyed. Buildings were flattened. The few that remained were black from the fires and smoke. People's hard-earned possessions littered the street.

My stomach turned, and I could taste the smoke in my throat again, even though it was long gone. In my mind, I could hear the shots being fired, and I fought the urge to duck.

Tears stung my eyes and rolled hot down my cheeks. *How could anyone have enough hate in their hearts to do this to people?* I couldn't imagine it. Especially with no reason at all to hate them.

We separated into smaller groups and silently headed in different directions. Cora and I squeezed each other's hands. We were all going to check on our homes.

The closer we got, the more the maggots in my stomach wiggled. I worked hard not to vomit.

Finally, we stood in front of what used to be our house.

"Oh no," I whispered, starting to cry.

All that was left of our house was half of the living room wall, and it was black from the flames and smoke. I couldn't even recognize the rest. The walkway that used to lead to our porch now led to a pile of black ruins.

Mama crumbled to the ground and sobbed. Cora sat next to her and hugged her. I took Daddy's hand and watched tears roll down his cheeks. There was nothing but ashes where his roses used to be.

I don't know how long we stayed in front of our burned-down house. It seemed like time stopped. Eventually, Daddy let go of my hand and lifted Mama up off the ground. She leaned into him and covered her face.

"What will we do?" asked Mama.

"We'll rebuild it," said Daddy. "That's all we can do."

"But it's all gone," she said.

I slipped my hand into Mama's. "No, Mama," I said. "We're still here."

Daddy smiled down at me. "Indeed we are," he agreed.

We walked until we found a spot where people from our group were setting up tents. People from the Red Cross were there too.

One man said, "Most of Mount Zion is gone, but the basement is still there. We can make use of that and build it back up."

"Booker T. Washington High School is still standing," said another.

The first man said, "Well, if that isn't a sign, I don't know what is."

Mama and Cora smiled at each other.

"My legal practice will set up a tent," said a tall man in a suit. "We'll get started figuring out what we can get done through the courts."

A murmur went through the crowd as people shared what they could do. Everyone seemed excited about helping.

Daddy said, "Tomorrow, we can start salvaging whatever we can from the home sites. There's bound to be things we can use."

An older woman nodded. "If we built it once, we can do it again."

Daddy nodded. "Booker T. Washington didn't call us Negro Wall Street for nothing," he said.

"Amen," said some of the people in the crowd.

Daddy winked at me, and I knew that even though things were horrible, they weren't hopeless. It wouldn't be this way forever.

"Amen," I said.

A NOTE FROM
THE AUTHOR

The land on which the Greenwood District of Tulsa,
Oklahoma, was built was originally inhabited by the
Cherokee, Chickasaw, Choctaw, Creek, and Seminole
tribes. They had been forced from their homelands by
white settlers. The tribes brought enslaved Africans
with them. After slavery ended, some of the Black
citizens stayed and lived among the Native American
tribes. When the government allotted land to the tribes,
Black Americans were able to own land.

Word spread that these communities were safe places
for Black people, and more began to arrive. Successful
Black businesspeople from other states came to Tulsa.
One of the first was O.W. Gurley, who bought forty
acres of land. He built his own businesses, but he also
provided loans to Black people. They bought portions
of the land to start businesses and build homes.

In this way, Greenwood grew in population, success,
and reputation. It attracted Black people looking for

safety, opportunity, and education. It boasted numerous Black-owned businesses, including schools, libraries, hotels, theaters, law offices, stores, and restaurants. Those who didn't work in Greenwood worked for white people in Tulsa, but they lived and spent their money in Greenwood.

In 1913, Booker T. Washington gave Greenwood the nickname "Negro Wall Street of America" because of its flourishing businesses and economy. Born a slave, Washington was freed after the Civil War and went on to found Tuskegee University, a Black college, as well as the Negro Business League. He was the first Black person to be invited to the White House, and he advised Presidents Theodore Roosevelt and William Howard Taft.

Over time, Washington's nickname for Greenwood was updated to "Black Wall Street," and by 1921, the district was home to nearly 10,000 Black people. They had found their own way to grow a successful economy. This success made the white people of Tulsa angry and jealous. When Dick Rowland was accused of assaulting Sarah Page, white Tulsans felt it gave them the excuse they were looking for to attack Greenwood.

Today, we know that Rowland was innocent. He did not assault Sarah Page in the elevator of the Drexel Building. Most people believe he tripped over the uneven elevator landing and bumped into her. In fact, Page didn't press charges, and by the end of September 1921, Rowland was declared innocent.

It is estimated that nearly 300 Black people were killed during the Tulsa Race Massacre. Hundreds more were injured. Thousands were left without homes. The property damage was thought to be almost $2 million—nearly $30 million today. According to the Red Cross, 1,256 homes were burned down, and 215 homes were looted but not destroyed.

Not one of the white people who participated in the massacre was punished. In fact, after the massacre, white Tulsans blamed the people of Greenwood. They claimed Black people had started it by coming to the courthouse to protect Rowland.

Meanwhile, thousands of Black citizens were detained like prisoners at the fairgrounds, McNulty Park, and the Convention Hall. Many were not let go unless a white employer came to get them. Some were held for weeks and forced to pay for their lodging and food.

Following the massacre, the government and officials tried to discourage the people of Greenwood from rebuilding. Insurance companies would not pay for lost property. Attempts were made by the government to take the land for their own use. Nothing could kill the spirit of the citizens of Greenwood, though. Greenwood's lawyers worked hard to fight the system. Many citizens stayed and rebuilt the community. Within days, the first new structures were already underway.

For many years, the story of the Tulsa Race Massacre wasn't told. The victims of the massacre didn't talk about it, and many believe the government and white Tulsans tried to keep it quiet. In recent years, however, survivors of the massacre have spoken out. Community organizations are educating people about what happened. Books for young people are being published. In Tulsa, memorial statues and plaques exist to honor what was lost and destroyed.

May 30, 2021, marked 100 years since the Tulsa Race Massacre, and finally, the silence has been broken.

Today, you can find books and recorded programs about Greenwood's history. There are exhibits in Tulsa available to the public. The truth is being told.

And so this book ends as it began. This can never happen again. The pattern of violence against Black people must stop. People must speak up for what is right. Like Lena and her family, we must be brave and persevere. What can *you* do to help end injustice?

MAKING CONNECTIONS

1. In Chapter Two, Lena encourages Daddy to leave with Mr. Wilson to protect Dick Rowland. Do you think that was good advice? Why or why not? Give evidence from the story to support your opinion.

2. Some citizens of Greenwood returned after the massacre while others never went back. What would you have done and why? Use facts from the foreword, story, and author's note to give reasons for your answer.

3. In the story, Daddy says, "Nothing ever changes." Think about the events leading up to and during the Tulsa Race Massacre in 1921. Then think about current events in America. Do you think things have changed? Why or why not? Using specific reasons and events from this story and real life, write 2 to 3 paragraphs to explain your opinion.

GLOSSARY

assault (ah-SAWLT)—a violent attack on another person

deputize (DEP-yuh-tahyz)—to give someone the power to do something in place of another person

fictionalize (FIK-shuh-nuh-lahyz)—to change a true story into fiction by changing or adding details

gossip (GOSS-ip)—talk or rumors about other people, often untrue and unkind

home guards (HOHM GAHRDS)—replacement guards organized in Tulsa to take the place of the National Guard who went to fight in World War I

loot (LOOT)—to steal from stores or houses during or after a disaster

lynch (LYNCH)—to be put to death, often by hanging, by mob action and without legal authority

massacre (MASS-uh-kuhr)—the needless killing of a group of helpless people

procession (pruh-SESH-uhn)—a group of people moving in an orderly, often ceremonial, way

salvage (SAL-vidge)—to recover something usable, especially from wreckage or ruin

segregated (SEG-ruh-gay-ted)—separated by race

sniper (SNY-pur)—a soldier trained to shoot at long-distance targets from a hidden place

Victrola (vik-TROH-luh)—a brand of record player

vigilante (vij-uh-LAN-tee)—a person who takes the law into his or her own hands and punishes others personally and illegally rather than relying on legal authorities

Wall Street (WAWL STREET)—a narrow street in New York City and the major financial center of the United States